For pea-ple everywhere—young and old, large and small, green and round

BEACH LANE BOOKS • An imprint of Simon & Schuster Children's Publishing Division • 1230 Avenue of the Americas, New York, New York 10020 • Copyright © 2010 by Keith Baker • All rights reserved, including the right of reproduction in whole or in part in any form. • BEACH LANE BOOKS is a trademark of Simon & Schuster, Inc. • For information about special discounts for bulk purchases, please contact Simon & Schuster Special Sales at 1-866-506-1949 or business@simonandschuster.com. • The Simon & Schuster Speakers Bureau can bring authors to your live event. For more information or to book an event, contact the Simon & Schuster Speakers Bureau at 1-866-248-3049 or visit our website at www.simonspeakers.com. • Book design by Sonia Chaghatzbanian • The text for this book is set in Frankfurter Medium. • The illustrations for this book are rendered digitally. • Manufactured in China • 0110 SCP • 10 9 8 7 6 5 4 3 2 • Library of Congress Cataloging-in-Publication Data • Baker, Keith, 1953– • LMNO peas / Keith Baker.—1st ed. • p. cm. • Summary: Busy little peas introduce their favorite occupations, from astronaut to zoologist. • ISBN 978-1-4169-9141-0 (hardcover : alk. paper) • [1. Stories in rhyme. 2. Peas—Fiction. 3. Occupations—Fiction. 4. Alphabet.] I. Title. II. Title: L M N O peas. • PZ8.3.B175Lm 2010 • [E]—dc22 • 2009012672

Keith Baker

LMNO peas

Beach Lane Books New York London Toronto Sydney

We are peas—alphabet peas!
We work and play in the ABCs.

We're acrobats,

and astronauts in space.

artists,

We're builders,

bathers,

and bikers in a race.

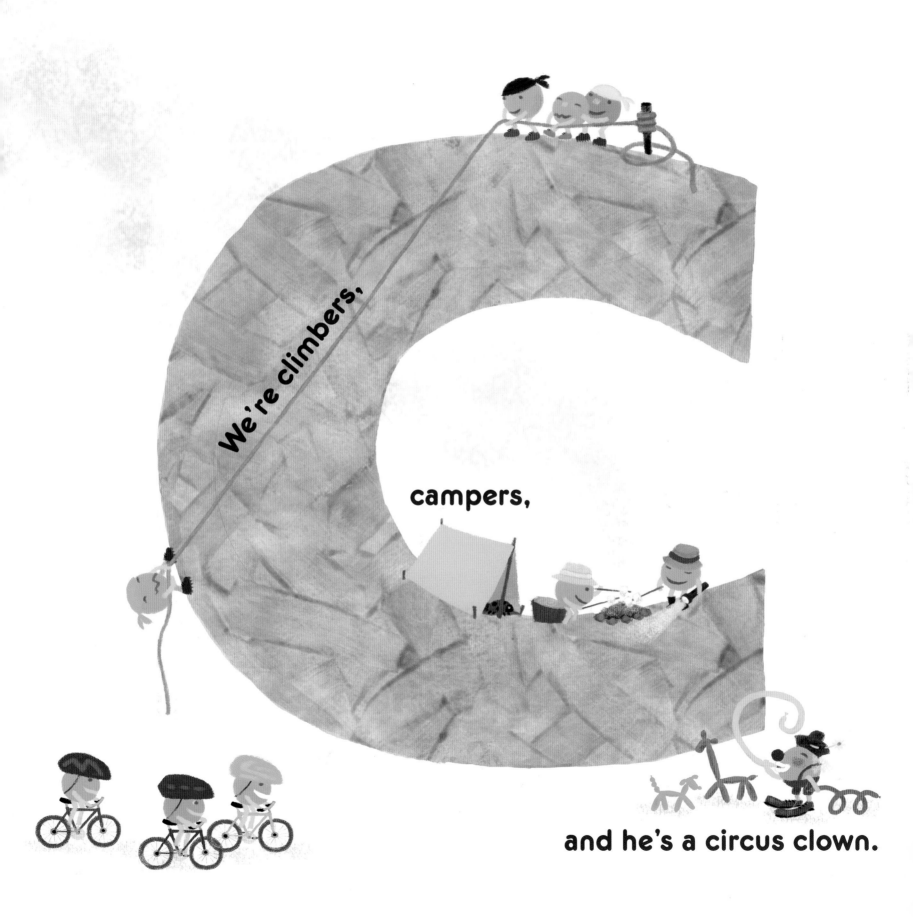

We're climbers,

campers,

and he's a circus clown.

We're dancers—

Can you dig it?

and drivers round town.

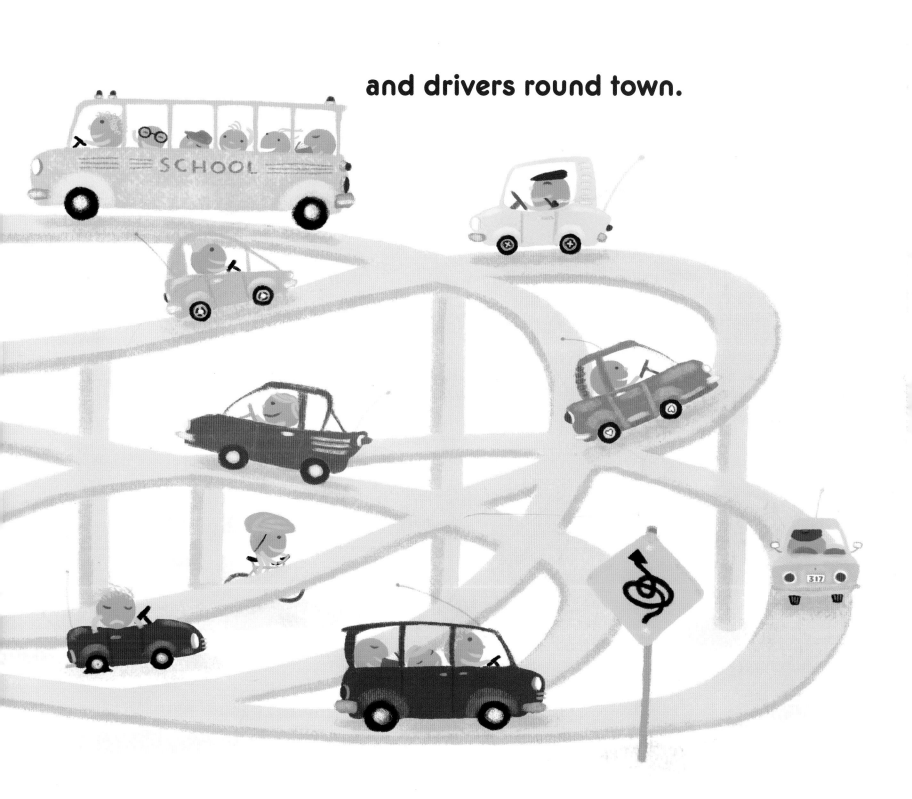

We're eaters,

electricians,

and explorers searching land.

We're farmers,

flaggers,

and best friends in a band.

We're gardeners,

gigglers,

givers and takers.

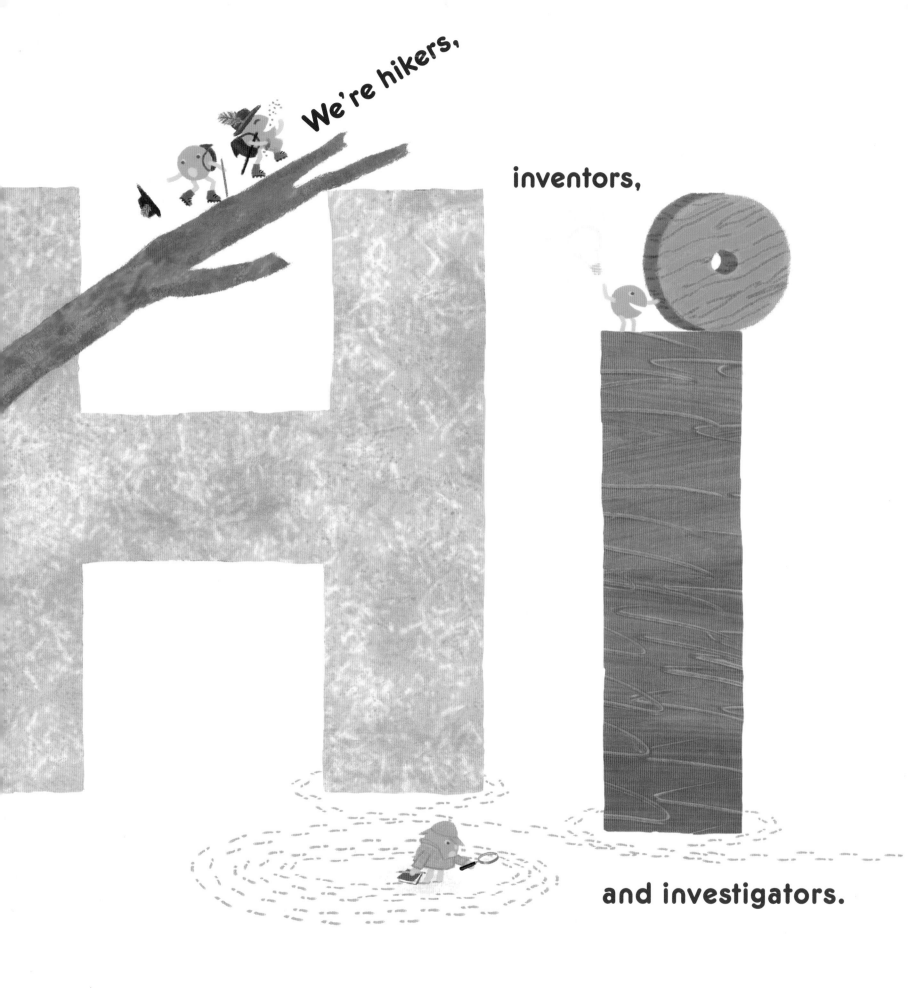

We're hikers, inventors, and investigators.

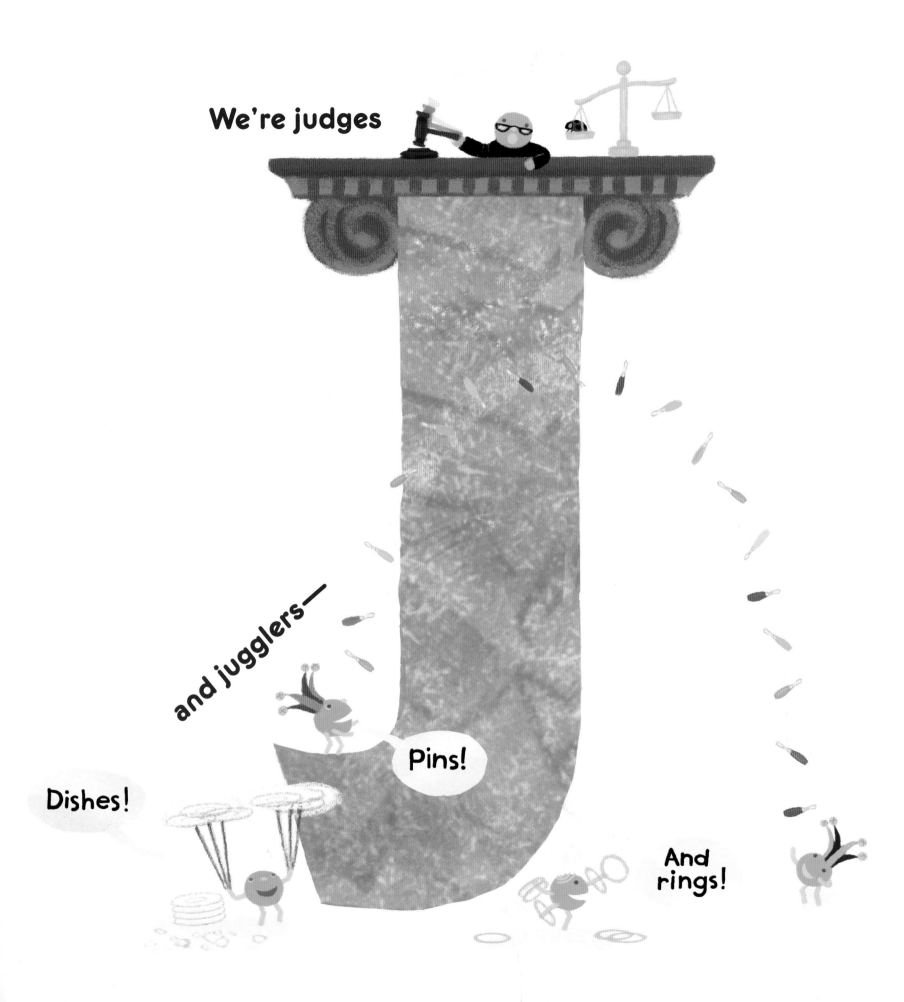

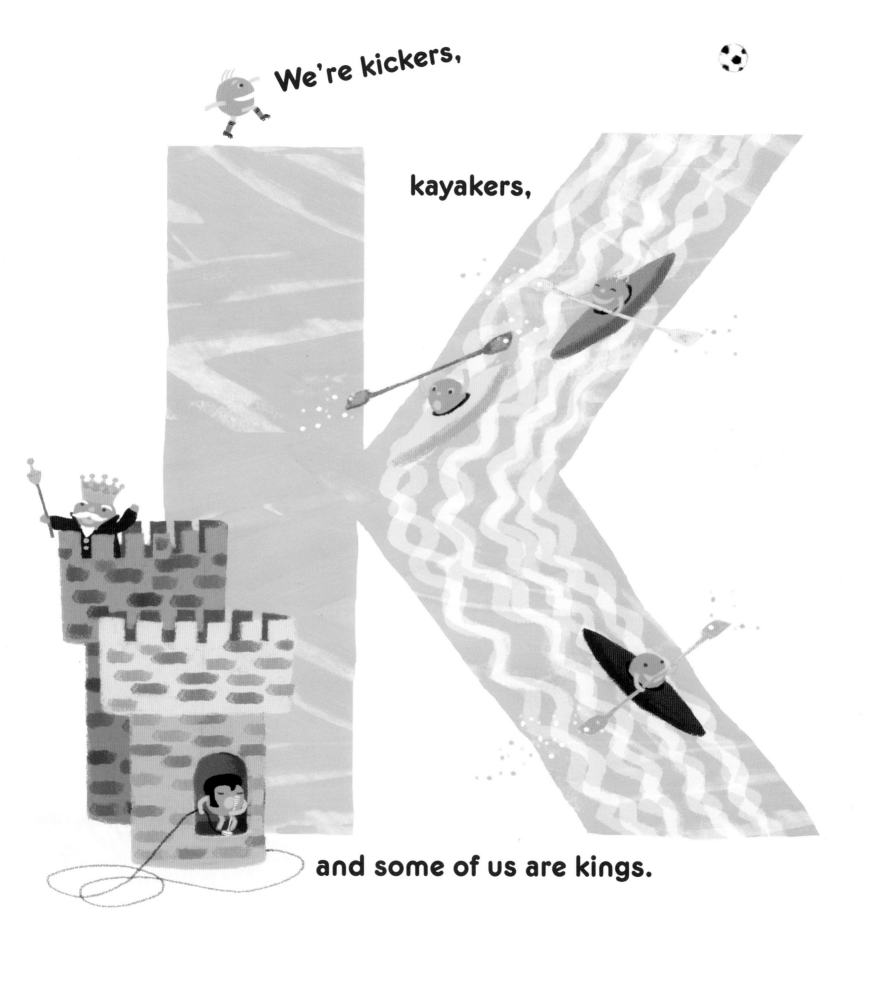

We're listeners,

miners,

and neighbors right next door.

We're nurses, officers,

and outlaws taking more.

We're painters,

poets,

and plumbers fixing leaks.

We're pilots,

parachutists,

we're peas and . . .

we're unique!

We're quilters,

quarterbacks,

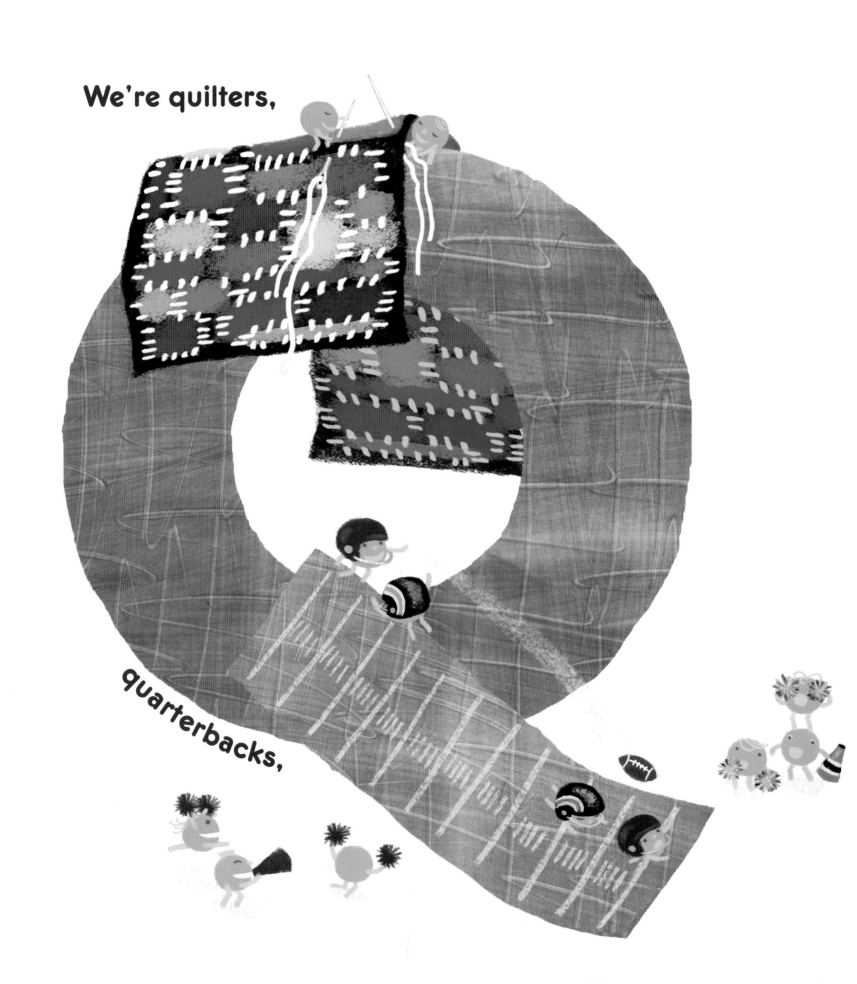

and readers—

Next page,
please.

We're scientists,

and sailors on the seas.

swimmers,

We're truckers,

teachers—

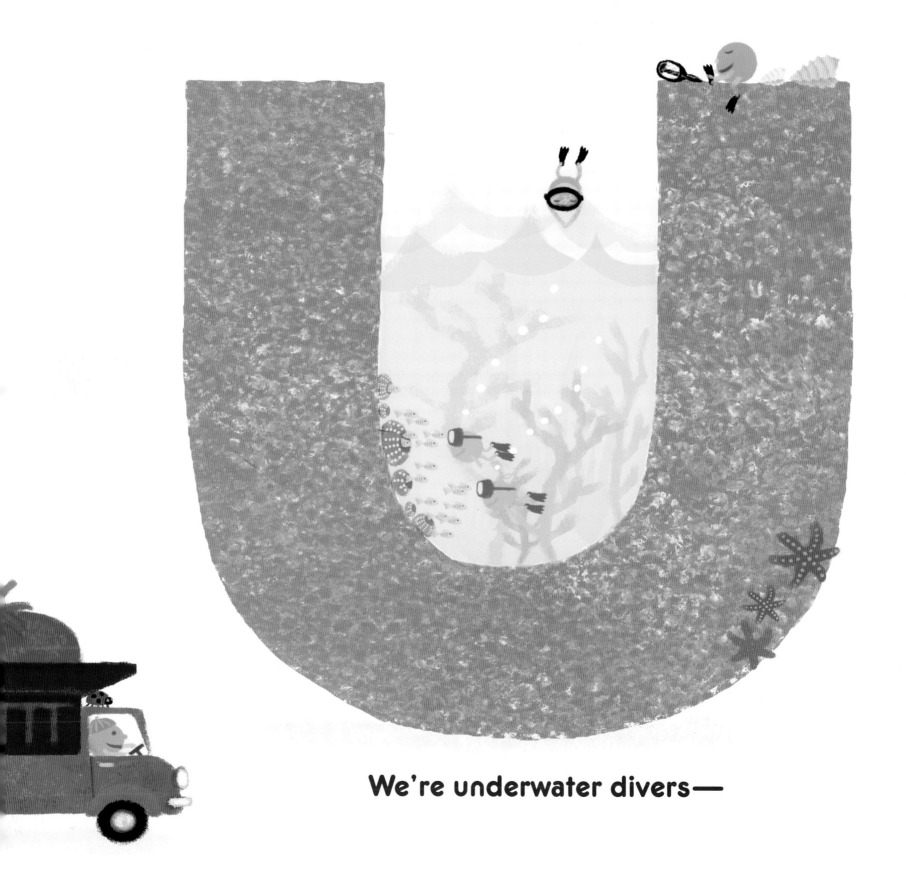

We're underwater divers—

voters,

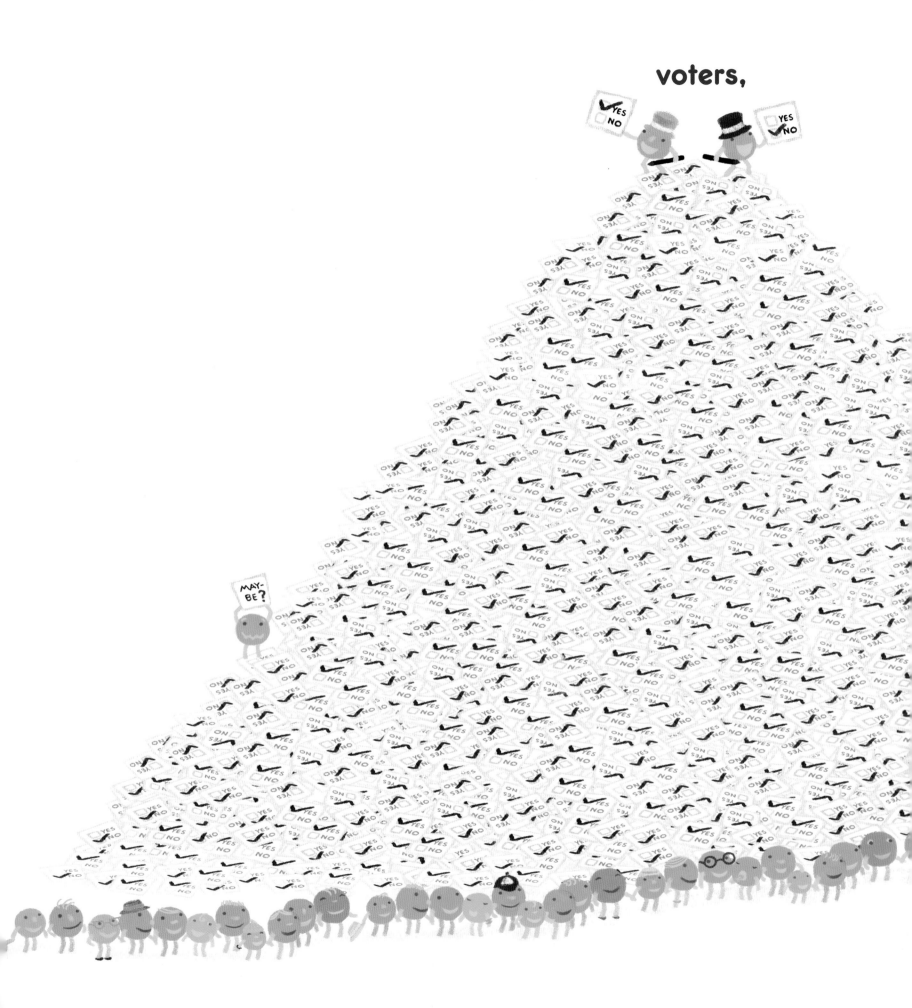

vets,

and volunteers.

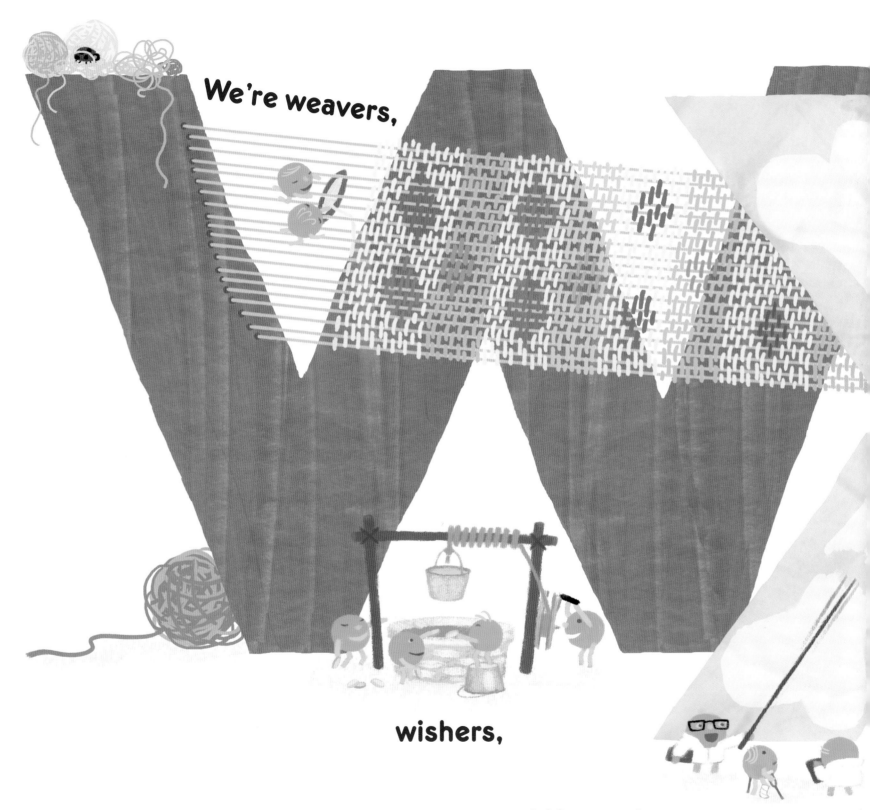

We're weavers,

wishers,

and X-ray doctors, too.

We're yogis
in a pose, and . . .

zoologists—that's who!

We are peas from A to Z.
Now tell us, please . . .